Teasel & Twigs
'TIS A CRITTER CHRISTMAS TALE

Paige DD Singer & Robert Dionne

Wilmington, Delaware

Teasel & Twigs
'Tis a Critter Christmas Tale

Second Printing 2013

Published by:
Cedar Tree Books, Ltd.
Wilmington, Delaware 19807
books@ctpress.com
www.cedartreebooks.com

ISBN 978-1-892142-54-2

Title: Teasel & Twigs, 'Tis a Critter Christmas Tale
Author: Paige DD Singer
Illustrator: Robert Dionne
Editor: Nick Cerchio
Copy Editor: Beverly Cerchio
Book Design: Bob Schwartz

Library of Congress Cataloging-in-Publication Data

Singer, Paige DD.
Teasel & Twigs : 'tis a Critter Christmas Tale / by Paige DD Singer ; illustrations, Robert Dionne. -- First edition.
     pages cm
ISBN 978-1-892142-54-2 (alk. paper)
I. Dionne, Robert. II. Title. III. Title: Teasel and Twigs.
PZ8.3.S6158Te 2012
[E]--dc23
                        2012036024

Printed and bound in the United States of America

Dedication

... with never-ending gratitude to the creative minds
of the Brandywine River Museum Volunteers
who bring Critters to life every year.
And a special thanks to the Wyeth family
whose characters and talent inspire our children to wonder.
Lastly, thanks to Rand Singer, who sparked the idea
and steadfastly shepherded us through this Critter adventure.

Foreword

It's a thought that washed over me and made me sad. My children will not remember my Gram. They remember her now, but time will eventually fill their young minds with other adventures, now that she is gone. But she is worth remembering. Their great-grandmother, Libby Dean, was full of creativity, character and charm. I want them to know she had perfectly shaped, polished pink nails covered with dirt, glue and paint, thanks to years spent creating Critters for Christmas on the Brandywine. Around the holidays, she sported a beautiful balance of gritty earth and bold earrings. I want my children to imagine her sage green art table, covered with a bric-a-brac of dried nature and freshly glued Critter

figures. I wish for them to feel at home in the Brandywine River Museum, as my brother and I did because of hours spent meandering through the collections with her. I want to see them wave a hello to Den Den, Jamie's pig, and to wonder, if you look closely and long enough, will Andrew's yellow lab be breathing? Living so far away in Arizona now, I need to know I can connect them to her creative world and the community of my childhood. I will write a poem bringing life to her art, her Critters. I know my children won't remember her, but my hope is that they will always know her character through her Critters. It's a thought that washed over me and made me smile.

Paige DD Singer

Teasel & Twigs

'Tis a Critter Christmas Tale

'Twas a night on the Brandywine, all through the halls,
Every Critter awoke to find pine tree lined walls.
"It's tomorrow! The party!" They sang out with joy,
While they fluffed the soft milkweed and buffed each new toy.

But one reindeer was sad, downright gloomy, forlorn.
For you see, he had lost his most prized peppercorn.
"Oh, my nose! It is gone!" Roger huffed with a frown.
"I will not look my best," and a tear trickled down.

So down rushed his close Critter friends, Teasel and Twigs,
A wise hare and young owl, with a curious jig.

"To the Gingerbread man, he will grant us a tour!
We will find one among all the cookies. I'm sure!"

They slid down the pipe banister, fast as a flurry.
But the Gingerbread man waved 'em on in a hurry,
"The old train engineer on the second floor tracks
Has a cargo of trinkets and Christmas knickknacks."

So they scurried the banister, racing the night.
The man said, "I am sorry. Head up! One more flight!
From the Ark, the giraffe might just spot your lost wear.
He's a Critter with height and so sharp a broad stare."

So they flew up the stairwell, a'huffing and puffing.
As the time neared an end and their friends were done fluffing,

"Hurry Teasel and Twigs!" was the chant they both heard,
Swiftly scampering sounds over cheers of each word.

Both were tired but encouraged,
they chose to push on.
The giraffe looked around
with a worry toward dawn.

"No luck here." He then sighed,
not to see what they're after.
"And the night is soon passing.
It's time now to gather."

Twigs and Teasel, heads hung, feeling lost, not so bold,
Slid downstairs, heavy-hearted... but lo, and behold!
The museum was wondrous with moonlit bright sights.
All the trimmings from nature were twinkling with light!

They found Roger, their deer friend, in much better spirits.
The sad news of his nose? He refused, would not hear it!
"It is not that important to look less than grand,
Just as long as my family and friends are at hand."

So spread cheering throughout the fine art in the hall.
It was jolly and festive, a jubilant ball.
Twigs then jumped and he jigged, a new thought in his head.
Off he swooped and then soaring, he snatched something red.

He flew back, with a holly branch clamped in his beak.
Then he plucked off a berry, and turned 'round to speak,
"Though it's not a black pepper, perhaps this will do.
A red-rosy and jovial nose just for you!"

The deer sprang, so delighted. He bounced and he pranced.
All the Critters applauded with joy, now entranced.
Twigs gazed wide, truly awed, acorn eyes all agleam.
Then he frolicked on down, glad to join the night's dream.

An ethereal angel flew down from above,

She touched Twigs and then Teasel and smiled, full of love.
Then called 'round with an echo all Critters could hear,
"The museum looks brilliant, a wonder this year!

Reminisce on this night. Everyone should feel proud."
Then she rose, with a wink, to a goat's-beard fluffed cloud,
But called down from the tree before fading from sight,
"Merry Christmas to all. Peace and love for all nights!"

'Til the next adventure...

About the Author & Illustrator

PAIGE DD SINGER

Photographed holding an heirloom Angel Critter crafted by her grandmother, Paige DD Singer, a native of Chadds Ford, Pennsylvania, now lives with her husband, Jason Furedy, and two children, Asher and Gundry in Phoenix, Arizona.

When not perfecting her role of *Domestic Goddess*, she enjoys exploring the prickly nooks and crannies of Arizona's sparse and arid wilderness, where she often ponders the idea of desert critters.

ROBERT DIONNE

Robert Dionne lives in Chadds Ford, PA with his wife and two children.

"I enjoyed the experience of illustrating this book and did not want it to end. It was an honor and joy bringing the Critters to life and celebrating Christmas with them every day in my studio."

www.robertdionneartist.com

Colophon

Teasel & Twigs: 'Tis a Critter Christmas Tale was designed in Italy by Bob Schwartz on an Apple MacPro using Adobe InDesign and Photoshop CS6. Titles were set in Cochin LT Std and Bodoni. The text was set in sixteen point Cochin LT Std nineteen point leaded.

Cochin is a transitional serif typeface that was originally produced in 1912 by Georges Peignot for the Paris foundry Deberny & Peignot and was based on the copperplate engravings of French artist Nicolas Cochin from which the typeface also takes its name. In 1977 Cochin was adapted and expanded by Matthew Carter for Linotype. Bodoni is a serif typeface first designed by Giambattista Bodoni in 1798.

The first edition of this book was digitally printed and bound in the United States of America by Total Printing Systems, Inc. of Newton, Illinois on 100# white smooth text.